Our Lives Became Unmanageable

Our Lives Became Unmanageable

Jackie Craven

OMNIDAWN PUBLISHING
RICHMOND, CALIFORNIA
2016

Cover art adapted from painting *The Dream #2* by Louise Hourrigan (the author's mother), oil on canvas, 30" x 30", © Copyright 1990, all rights reserved.

Cover text set in Cronos Pro and Garamond Pro
Interior text set in Bernhard Modern and Garamond Pro

Cover and Interior Design by Ken Keegan

Offset printed in the United States
by Edwards Brothers Malloy, Ann Arbor, Michigan
On 55# Heritage Book Cream White Antique
Acid Free Archival Quality Recycled Paper

Library of Congress Cataloging-in-Publication Data

Names: Craven, Jackie, author.
Title: Our lives became unmanageable / Jackie Craven.
Description: Oakland, California : Omnidawn Publishing, 2016.
Identifiers: LCCN 2016028857 | ISBN 9781632430274 (pbk. : alk. paper)
Classification: LCC PS3603.R392 O97 2016 | DDC 813/.6--dc23
LC record available at https://lccn.loc.gov/2016028857

Published by Omnidawn Publishing, Richmond, California
www.omnidawn.com   (510) 237-5472   (800) 792-4957
10 9 8 7 6 5 4 3 2 1
ISBN: 978-1-63243-27-4

Clara

I never would've gone to Porgett's if I'd known the mirrors in the changing room were defective. I leaned close to the glass but some disturbance interfered with my reflection. My face wobbled and blurred.

I tapped the mirror lightly. My smile fluttered, then went blank.

As you probably know, there's no privacy—no partitions and no curtains—in the changing room at Porgett's. On the day the mirrors gave out, a silver-haired woman in a satin slip stepped into a sequin evening gown. Her image glittered on the wall. Beside her, a teenager wearing feather earrings turned from side to side, puckered her lips, and frowned.

For these two women, the mirrors functioned perfectly. Bright glass reflected the silver-haired woman, reflected the girl with the feather earrings, and reflected the reflections of their reflections, which reflected the reflections of their reflected reflections, which reflected every wall, every bench, every detail in the room except for me.

I touched my face—as warm and solid as any human face. I'm short, with red hair and dark eyebrows. You might say I'm a bit plump, but not fat enough to break a mirror. I gave the glass another tap—first with the tips of my fingers, then sharply with my knuckles. My reflection crackled into focus (corkscrew hair gone crazy) and then—*poof.*

The silver-haired woman blinked. The girl ruffled her feather earrings. I felt air drain from the room. Had they noticed? "Damned mirrors," I muttered with a shrug. "So lazy and undependable."

"Never met a single one I could trust," the silver-haired woman responded graciously.

The feather-earring girl giggled. I started to giggle, too. Then the three of us laughed loud enough to jingle the wire hangers on the return rack. Stringed music drifted down from hidden speakers—a tune from that Audrey Hepburn movie about the moon and the jewelry store. The lyrics are still on the tips of my ears.

Angelo

See that cloud? It's mine. I stood on the roof of my apartment building and stopped it before it could glide by. It was a fluffy, cumulus cloud—the only one in an unusually blue sky.

I'd gone to the roof to get away from my mother. Day in, day out, she trailed after me, a scrap of paper caught on my shoe. *Angelo. When are you gonna get a job? When are you gonna get married?* Then, like I was ten, *When are you gonna clean your room?*

Up on the roof, I felt far away from her and everything else. Our building is nine stories high, the tallest on Erie Boulevard. Heat vents sprout like silver mushrooms on top. Sitting on one of the mushrooms, I could see over the rim of Porgett's Department Store. Matchbox trucks puttered around the locksmith shop. The neon sign on top of the GE Plant became a hula hoop. When I closed my eyes, cars swished like an ocean.

The ocean—that's where I belonged. Living on grilled swordfish and salt breezes. Here on the roof, the air smelled like tar. The tar sucked at my sneakers when I walked to the edge.

No, I didn't plan to jump. I just wanted to watch ant-sized people swirl through the spinning glass doors at Porgett's. *Angelo, don't you have nothing better to do?* My mother's voice was an engine revving in my head. If she had her way, I'd apply for that opening in ladies shoes. I'd sign up for their retirement plan. I'd marry a girl with big eyebrows.

Then I got this feeling. Like I had company on the roof. When I turned, something moved. Not my mother, but something. The cloud. Right there, not ten feet away, behind a silver dome.

This was, as I've said, a lumpy, formless cloud. A blob of white against amazing blue. I inched closer. If I looked sideways—first with one eye, then with the other—I detected shapes. A dancer, a werewolf, an old man in a chair.

Maybe I heard things, too. Cloud whispers—wispy water sounds telling me that my life also had a shape. Foggy, sure, but interesting. And complicated. Definitely not the shape of a shoe clerk. Clear as sunshine, I saw an artist—a visionary like Rembrandt or Van Gogh or Picasso, which explained why my mother didn't get me. Artists are complicated. But that's okay because artists are immortal, too.

When the cloud drifted closer, I pulled it in. The smell of melting tar gave way to suntan lotion. Such a fragrant cloud, with a slightly salty flavor. Like sea-foam.

But slippery! When I patted the mist, it scooted from me. I lunged to catch it. "Hold on, hold on there."

The cloud settled down a bit, but still trembled. I stroked it ever so softly, ever so patiently.

Not just anyone can sculpt clouds. You have to have vision to see the potential that hides inside. You have to have skill to keep it from slithering between your fingers. Beneath my touch, the cloud relaxed and became pliable. With a sweep of my hand—a Mona Lisa smile. With a flick of my wrist—the hollow of a woman's cheek. A nudge of my thumb—depth, texture. *Complexity.*

After an hour, vapor shimmered before me. My clothes were soaked. She was beautiful.

Later, I tried to show my mother. She eyed me suspiciously, then squinted up. *Cloud sculptures? How? Where?* All she could see were wisps drifting toward the horizon. *Honestly, Angelo. When will you ever get a job?*

Clara

In those days, I wrote advertising copy for the Chandler store, on the top level of the shopping mall. After the fuss with the mirrors, when I didn't need any extra stress, Gifford requested an ad for a new line of Aerialist shoes. *Bouncy? Buoyant?* Just try to find words for the weird, silvery soles. *Luminescent?* Gifford shook his bald head. "Can't you make the slogan stronger?"

Gifford planned to fire me. I felt his anger roll in, as predictable as the tide. I brought the sample shoes home, slipped them on, and flopped from room to room. These shoes were huge. *Expansive? Bountiful?*

My mind felt empty as the antique mirror over my dressing table.

Sarah

So I go to his apartment just like usual and there my father is, stuck to the ceiling like a housefly. "Daddy," I cry. "Are you all right?"

Daddy doesn't say anything right away. He gulps from his coffee mug, holding it with both hands to keep from spilling. Then he wipes his mouth with his sleeve and sets the mug on one blade of the ceiling fan.

"A bit of trouble with my gravity today," Daddy says.

Well I should've known this would happen. Daddy was a thin man, and short. Seemed like the only thing that held him down were those heavy boots he wore. Anywhere he went, he held onto walls and railings, like he knew he'd go flying into space if he wasn't careful. And now it's happening. My daddy's on the ceiling, with no one but me to keep him from whirling off into never-never land.

"You didn't eat that pot of stew I made, did you?" I find the pot in the refrigerator and it's still mostly full. After warming it up, I stand on a chair and spoon-feed my father. He takes the stew willingly enough, but chews slowly, staring down at me with dark, resentful eyes.

"No more gravity," he says.

"You'll be fine," I tell him. "You just need to put on some weight."

Spoon by spoon, my father eats nearly the whole pot. He eats so much he has to let out a notch in his belt. But he doesn't drop one inch from the ceiling.

"When a man's gravity goes, it goes," he tells me.

"Don't you worry, Daddy," I say. "I'll get you down from there even if I have to tie you down."

There's plenty of clothesline strung from pulleys outside his window, so I draw in the rope, fold his laundry, and tether my father to a kitchen chair. The chair, being made of aluminum, floats up and Daddy's head smacks against the ceiling. He glowers.

"Can't you see my gravity is gone?"

"Never you mind." This time I tie him to his wingback armchair. I wrap the clothesline three times around the big claw feet.

Daddy scowls. "I'm not a wild elephant, you know."

I remind him that being tied to a chair is a long sight better than bobbing around on the ceiling. And I tell him that the rope is only temporary. All he needs is a bit more weight on him. Then I feed him oatmeal with butter and heavy cream, mashed potatoes slathered with gravy, and a spoonful of cake frosting, fresh out of the can.

After several hours of heavy eating, Daddy turns his face from me. "I'm not a child."

People can be so unappreciative, especially family. One day I come with groceries only to find no chair, no clothesline, no

Daddy. A breeze blows in through the open window. I turn to look and there he is. Still tied to that ratty old chair, he cleaves to the underbelly of a low-hanging cloud.

"Daddy!" The clothesline dangles like a kite string just beyond the window ledge. Stretching for it, I manage to grasp a frayed end. "I got you—"

I do my damnedest to reel him in, but the wind pulls hard, tugging Daddy and his chair toward the smokestacks and dragging me, still holding tight, half out the window. He's no help at all. Kicking his feet and paddling his arms, he shouts, "Dang you, girl, won't you just let go?"

I promise I'll hold on, no matter what. Then I feel my knees scrape against the sill and I hear the whoosh of traffic below and I think, *Lordy, I'm gonna fall.* As I fling out my arms to catch myself, the rope slips away. The chair with my daddy turns three lazy somersaults and drifts beyond my reach.

The silly old man doesn't even holler for help. Soaring over rooftops and bouncing across clouds, all he says is, "*Wheeeeeeeeee!*"

Monique

Sure, the rope is narrow. That's not what makes walking it so hard. It's the height—the staring down so far and seeing faces stare back like so many fried eggs. No sound up there.

You don't hear the monkey playing its calliope or the Clydesdale horses shuffling their oversized hooves. Even the babies, long overdue for their naps, hold their breath. Suspended in all that silence, mingled with the scent of popcorn and elephant dung, you step, balance, step, balance. The balance swings inside you like a pendulum.

Even so, you imagine a missed step, the sensation of empty air. You see your bare foot groping for the rope, you see your arms spinning and your legs peddling, you see yourself twirling like a maple seedling, tutu over your ears. The scene spools through your mind in slow motion, a silent film with flickering shadows and tumbling dust and then a blinding white light.

You shut your eyes. You forget there is a net.

Clara

Nights and weekends, I practiced in front of my vanity mirror. It reflected the octagon pattern on my grandmother's quilt, the Tiffany lamp, magazines on the floor. No eyes, no nose, no mouth. Even when I pressed close, the glass saw through me to the round face of my bedside clock. I stared into the mirror, reading backwards time. *Bed. Lamp. Magazines. Clock.*

I tried the bathroom mirror, too, and the long mirror on the door to the hall closet, always with the same results. How strange and disturbing that everywhere I turned, mirrors malfunctioned, one after the other—like having every appliance in your house break, simultaneously. It was as though the mirrors had singled me out specifically, as though they made a conscious decision to exclude me.

Sliding along my bedroom wall, I crouched out of view. *Bed. Lamp. Magazines. Clock.* I leaped, landing before the mirror with outstretched arms. *Bed. Lamp. Magazines. Clock.*

Crouching again, I counted under my breath. Yes, it had come to this. I was a child playing hide-and-seek. At the count of ten, I flexed my knees and jumped. My finest cheerleader leap—You'd think this would be enough to jolt the universe. *Bed. Lamp. Magazines. Clock.*

I stood at my apartment window. I watched cars whizzing past and pedestrians bustling along the sidewalk looking diligent and purposeful in the halogen glow of the streetlamps. They could probably see themselves in every spotted mirror, and in silver trays, too, and in black glass and still ponds, in anything reflective.

Whirling, I raced the full length of my apartment—kitchen, living room, hall, bedroom, bathroom. I stopped in front of the medicine cabinet. Tubes of lipstick glistened on a glass shelf behind the half-open door. I imagined pink voices chanting, *You'll never wear us again.*

Regret sank into my hollows, a penny down a well. Isn't that the way? You never miss things until they're gone.

Rita

Just past midnight, I jolted awake to discover Francis had stolen my soul. I sat up with a groggy cry. "Where—?"

My husband sprawled like a figure in an El Greco painting—green-skinned, unnaturally long. I lay beside him and felt the hollow space inside me. I probed it the way a tongue pushes against a missing tooth. "Francis—!"

Frustration made my voice shrill. He stirred. Beautiful dark eyelashes fluttered. Then he sighed and nestled down. I slipped from bed and stepped barefooted across the linoleum floor. I opened the top drawer to his chest. On one side, socks were rolled like snails. The other side had folded underwear. Tucked between the socks and the underwear—a glass ashtray filled with pennies cold as death.

I shivered and closed the drawer. From the next room, a cricket chirped. No. Not a cricket. A bird or—such a high, pleading cry! My soul. I followed it down the hall into the living room. Maybe Francis had tucked my soul between the pages of a book. This was the sort of thing he might do. Yes, he would press it like a wildflower and expect praise for preserving it so well.

A streetlamp glowed through the window, lighting his Chippendale desk. A carved angel perched on top and beneath the angel were glass doors, steel key in the lock. I pulled out a magazine and flipped through pages.

Now the squeal shrilled like an emergency warning signal on the radio. The sound seemed to come from inside the desk where a labyrinth of pigeonholes held all our important papers. In the first hole—his paycheck stubs. These I tossed overhead like ticker tape. The second hole held the stubs to my paychecks—smaller than his. These I also tossed aside, along with the contents of the third and fourth holes— receipts for the renovations we'd done on our house. In the fifth hole—bank statements. Canceled checks spilled out— blue, green, pink.

All the while—that pitiful squealing! Reaching into the sixth and seventh holes, I pulled out the credit card bills and I flung these to the floor, too, and I grabbed the insurance papers from the eighth hole and hurled them aside, and I pulled letters with foreign stamps from the next three holes and I threw these right and left, and still the cry went on and on.

The twelfth pigeonhole was empty. I reached to my elbow. Our life together had fallen in drifts around my legs. Shuffling through papers, I returned to the bedroom. Sheets tangled around my husband's feet. His arms sprawled in a crucifixion pose. I lay beside him and listened to the squeal of my soul. It sang in tune with his breathing.

Shutting my eyes, I tried to breathe with him. *In, out. In, out.* Before long, I was dreaming of pigeons—a dozen of them, their purple feathers ruffled with fear. Flapping silent wings, they hovered overhead and watched me with bright black eyes. I sat up and held out a finger like a perch. If I could only be quiet, if I could only be still, the pigeons would see that I was safe, and the one who was mine would come.

Silence was the secret.

Kevin

I couldn't sleep that night. I pushed my head into the pillow, but couldn't block the light that seeped through the window shades. Plus, my wife, Nadine, had the TV in the living room turned high—Audrey Hepburn at full volume.

The light came from the moon, and the moon was almost full. Even though the shades were drawn, I could tell that this was a pale and lopsided moon—liquid around the rim, melting like an ice cube. I sat up. What harm could come from one glance?

Nadine has always been peculiar about the moon. Even when we were young, she nagged. Fifteen years of nagging and I made all kinds of promises. But now she was deep in her movie. And the moon—that sharp, metallic scent!

Just a whiff. Why not? The moon tugged at my marrow, pulled me toward the window. Audrey Hepburn sang *Moon River* in the living room. Outside, the pavement glowed. I felt my nostrils flair. Molten dreams. Scent of heaven.

The moon was, as I had imagined, wobbly, but not weak. No, this was a sweet, plump moon—swelling, juicy, and nearly ripe. My gums ached, remembering the taste of moons like this. And the light! It flowed like first love, like teenage sex, like God. *This is it! This is all!* I wanted to dance around the room, to leap through the window and gallop four-legged up the silver street. I'd bound over parked cars, I'd flee to the wooded park where—

A part of me wondered what Nadine would say. The other part of me reached for the latch. It snapped open easily enough, but the window jammed. I pressed my face against the glass. The back of my neck prickled with the sensation of hair coiling to the surface. From the next room Nadine called, "*Kevin—?*"

My tongue lolled, thick and heavy. I heard Nadine's slippers shuffle up the hall.

"*—Kevin?*"

I pushed at the window. By now my hands were clumsy, clawed things.

"*—Kevin!*"

I pounded the window. Nadine had bolted it. I hurled against the glass and when it shattered, I hopped onto the window ledge.

"Oh, Kevin," I heard her sigh. "Not again."

There was nothing she could say and nothing she could do that would keep me from leaping into that cold light. When it comes to the moon, I'm as helpless as the tide.

Clara

"Something luminescent," I told the salesman at Lord & Taylor.

"All our mirrors are of the finest glass." The salesman was one of those slender, blond types with sincere blue eyes. He touched my elbow. "Not like some other stores that sell shoddy products made of recycled materials."

"So many mirrors are defective," I said.

"Cheap labor. Made in China." His hand on my back, the salesman shepherded me to the grandest mirror I'd ever seen—tall and cherry-framed, crowned with cupids and garlands. "Now, this mirror is guaranteed. It will never darken or dim."

I wanted to inspect the glass, but when I approached, the mirror pivoted inside the frame and tilted toward the ceiling, beyond my view.

"Will it—?"

"Would I lie—?"

Julia

I drove sixteen hours to reach Delray, steaming from my ears. Finally, somewhere after exit 54, blind rage gave way to exhaustion and relief. I collapsed on the beach and watched the seagulls through half-closed eyes. Their rhythmic calls and the throb of the surf must have lulled me to sleep. By the time I woke, the sun was gliding west toward the Lobster Shanty and the volleyball nets. The sand had turned dark as whiskey. Amber streaks spilled from under my canvas bag and inched along the edge of the dunes.

Shaking my towel clean, I headed for the boardwalk. Maybe I'd splurge on a new swimsuit or a T-shirt with something philosophical written on it: *A woman needs a man like a fish needs a bicycle.* Better yet: *Never trust a man named Jim.*

Outside the bait shop, the boardwalk turned to slate. Not real slate—the color of slate, the color of soot, the color of thunder. Off-season tourists strolled from shop to shop wafting the scent of tanning lotion. The sun dipped lower. My rubber shoes slapped against my heels. *Take that! And that! And that!* Darkness grew taller by the hour.

~~~

Back at the hotel, I complained to the concierge.

"Madame, I assure you…" He was a tall, haughty man with arched eyebrows and a tired, mocking smile. He could have been my husband's twin. *Ex-husband's* twin. "Our beach is perfectly clean." Even his thin, nasal voice reminded me of Jim.

The next morning, the sun still pink, I returned to the beach. The tide had rolled back to reveal a wide stretch of muck. Gulls pecked at scraps of seaweed and spiraled overhead with their sad, screechy cries. In the swirl of feathers and sound, a woman with bare feet sat in a folding chair, a magazine open on her lap.

"Are you sure you want to sit there?" I asked. "It's the dirtiest spot."

"Really? Where?"

I held up my canvas tote. "I'll clean it."

"Well, goodness. I don't see anything, but I'll help if I can." The woman folded her chair and joined me in the sand, digging with bare hands. The sun burned and the darkness puddled around us. I shoved dirty sand into my tote bag and carried it to the trash barrel beneath the boardwalk. Then back again. And again and again.

"There now." The woman brushed her hands on her shorts. "Better?"

"Maybe." As the sun rose higher, the circle of darkness shrank like the pupil of an eye. I dumped another load of sand. "Yes! Yes, the beach *is* cleaner now."

"All problems should be so easy." The woman gathered her folding chair and her magazine. "I best go see if Henry's back from his swim. Who knows? Maybe he's home waiting for me."

"I've left my husband," I said. I wanted to tell the lifeguard, too, and I wanted to call out to the tourists on the boardwalk, and shout to the seagulls and the clouds: *I've left my husband! I've left my husband!*

Hungry for the first time in days, I sat beneath the red and white awning at the Lobster Shanty and ordered their famous lobster roll. The meat, moist with mayonnaise and lemon juice, melted in my mouth. The beach stretched out with the kind of blinding whiteness you only hope to see when you die. It was just that clean.

But, when the sun sank toward the row of hotels, dusky streaks stretched from the poles of the volleyball net and trailed after the tourists along the shore.

I went back to the beach, and this time I dug deeper. Water seeped into the holes I made. The blackness spilled around my hands, mixing with the water like blood. Lord knows what germs crept under my fingernails. My work took on a rhythm that matched the surf. *Dig, dump. Dig, dump.* Foam-flecked waves ebbed closer. They lapped the shore, spit up bits of seaweed, and swallowed.

"Why won't you help me?" I cried to no one in particular. The woman with the bare feet was long-gone. A lazy lifeguard slept in his high chair. Tourists in floppy hats scurried past. They didn't seem to notice the darkness that clung to their feet. A French poodle broke free from its owner's leash and pranced around me with delighted yips. The stain in the sand danced alongside him.

By dusk, the stains had swelled, spilling over broken shells and consuming what remained of the beach. I hurled another bagful into the garbage bin. A burst of seagulls swooped up from the tide. The darkness wasn't just in the sand. It was in the water, the sky, the clouds. I felt it settle over my shoulders like a damp embrace.

Breathing in my ear, it led me into the tide and pulled me toward the surf. Darkness in my mouth, darkness in my lungs. When I lunged for air, the darkness pulled me down. I lunged again, pushing against this thing that had no body, willing it to drown. It writhed, kicked, and went still— It did drown. Crashing to the surface, I threw back my head and swam for the clean, clean shore.

In my wake, the sly, dark thing—whatever it was—stirred to life. With synchronized strokes, it followed me onto the beach. I can't see it now. It hides behind the night. As soon as the sun rises, I'll find it beneath the pier or under a canvas umbrella, waiting like a patient lover.

Clara

Gifford was angry. I could tell by the note he left on my desk. His script looped downward across my memo pad. A negative turn of mind will cause words to dip like that, off the bottom edge. *Please see me...*

Gifford was going to fire me. Who could blame him? My shoe ads flopped. Three thousand Aerialists landed in the Dollar Store. And now, with my reflection behaving so erratically...

On the other hand, maybe Gifford planned to offer a raise. *Please.* The enormous *P* suggested Promise. After all, I'd been a loyal employee for over seven years. No...more than an employee. A friend. When his wife, Elizabeth, telephoned the office, didn't I chat with her, even though we'd never met? When their daughter, Julia, got married, didn't I send a silver place setting, even though I'd never had a wedding of my own? And, for creep's sake, why did Lord & Taylor deliver an enormous crate to his office? Weren't they supposed to send the cherry-framed mirror to *me*?

Nadine

Seven o'clock on a steamy August morning and the bell rings. The police, I think. Kevin's been arrested again. He's hurt someone. Or—

I fling the door open, but there's no police, no fireman, nobody official at all. Just Mrs. Knickerbocker, that funny lady from across the street, lugging her tapestry bag and hugging a damp bundle.

"Oh." I pull my robe closed.

Mrs. Knickerbocker blinks her raisin eyes, smiles at the bundle, and holds it out to me. Pale puffs of bread dough peek from a towel. "Give it ten days to rise," Mrs. Knickerbocker says. Before I can stop her, she tucks the bundle into my arms.

Startled, I try to find my tongue. How can I tell this woman that I've been up most of the night, that my husband is God knows where, and that I have no heart to fuss around the kitchen? The warm dough stirs against me, already rising. I force myself to smile. "It smells delicious."

Beaming, Mrs. Knickerbocker rattles off instructions—how often to knead the dough, how long to bake it, ingredients I can mix in. My head spins. For a moment I swear she's humming Christmas tunes—a cross between *Jingle Bells* and *Frosty the Snowman*, maybe with a splash of *Moon River*.

All this takes precious minutes. When Mrs. Knickerbocker finally leaves, I set her soggy gift in the kitchen sink and flick on the television. Any other day, the local news would report a grisly death or injury. But all the commentators want to talk about is that mess in Washington. Turning down the volume, I sit at the counter to make the necessary calls.

First I phone my office. "A touch of the flu," I say. "I'd come to work, but you don't want my germs. "

Then I call Kevin's foreman. "My husband is in agony. You shouldn't've asked him to carry that last load of lumber."

Then I call the True Value and order a new sheet of glass for the bedroom window. "Better make it tempered this time," I tell the clerk, who's been minding his store too many years to ask why our windows break so often.

Then I call the emergency room at St. Claire's.

"Yes—" The receptionist's voice is perky and hopeful. "We do have an unidentified male—"

I shut my eyes, thinking, *He's finally done it. He's killed someone, or*—I suck in my breath—*himself.* I imagine myself a widow like Mrs. Knickerbocker, living all alone in a house too big, baking bread, carrying oversized pocketbooks, and singing holiday songs out of season. Okay, I'll admit it. Mixed with the dread, there's a twinge of anticipation. Would a life like that be so terrible?

"They found him up north," the cheery receptionist goes on. "Young fellow, dove off a cliff."

31

"*Dove*?" Would Kevin do such a thing? "Do you mean *drove*?"

"No, *dove*. Can you believe it? A miracle he survived."

My husband could use a miracle. I pepper the receptionist with questions even though it's clear that the man in the hospital isn't Kevin. No one would mistake me or Kevin for *young*.

When I glance over at the sink, Mrs. Knickerbocker's dough has puffed so high, it seems to lap at the faucet. I nudge it to one side so I can pour water into the coffeepot. I stare blankly at the flickering television. I don't need to turn up the sound to know that the newsmen aren't talking about Kevin. The day weighs on me like a steamy towel and the rising bread sends out the heavy smell of yeast. When the pot begins to gurgle, I turn it off. What was I thinking? This day is too hot for coffee.

Despite the heat, I decide to wear my navy blue pantsuit. It's always best to look crisp and professional when you talk to police and I'm pretty sure I'll be meeting with them before this day is out. I wrap a red silk scarf around my neck. I check the bedroom mirror to make sure I don't look dowdy or desperate.

When Kevin and I met, we were both students. I was a drab little thing, an economics major. But Kevin—*Kevin*! He was a graduate student in the Music Department, a singer and saxophonist who could, with just a few notes, make even the

drunks set down their drinks. My roommate said there was
something strange, almost inhuman, about his voice. But her
worries had seemed silly and, anyway, it was Kevin's wildness
I loved.

So, here I am, driving around cul-de-sacs, slowing down
past houses with twirling lawn sprinklers, and heading west,
out into the country. The wide, flat road is empty. Everyone
has gone to the pool or the mall. When I see a child pumping
a bicycle along the shoulder, I roll down my window. "Have
you seen—?"

She pushes one sneaker into the yellow dust to stop the
bike. She's eleven or twelve, just beginning to grow breasts but
oblivious to them.

"He's not tall," I tell her, "but husky, and…"

Locusts in the field drown out my voice. Wiping a
platinum wisp of hair from her sunburnt face, the girl smiles
expectantly. Should I tell her that Kevin might be barefoot?
That he's wearing nothing but pajamas? I don't want to
frighten her. "He's harmless in the sunlight," I finally say. "But
do be careful, dear." Something about this girl shakes me.
She's so young. "You never know about strangers," I warn as I
pull away.

It's almost lunchtime. I'm not hungry, but know I should
eat something. I hurry home to find the message machine
empty. No one's phoned, not even Kevin's foreman to ask
whether he'll work tomorrow. I think about calling the

hospital again, think about calling the police, even think about calling Mrs. Knickerbocker—to say what? The words would catch in my throat like a lump of dough.

And speaking of dough, the aroma of it overpowers the kitchen. Mrs. Knickerbocker's gift now stretches the full length of the counter, slipping onto the floor at one end and, at the other end, pressing against the refrigerator and pushing off the magnets. *Fifty cents off, a dollar off, two-for-the-price-of-one*. All those discounts, scattered across the floor.

It's time I divided the dough into smaller loaves, but first I need to make a sandwich or a bowl of soup, but I can't get the cabinet doors open, and the dough has completely swallowed the microwave.

Unraveling the cord, I take the phone into the living room and sink into Kevin's wing-backed chair. Now I do call St. Claire's and the police and also the animal warden. There's still no word of Kevin, who's probably off making a fool of himself at some jazz café, or else he's hurt in some back alley, and there's nothing more for me to do except sweep up the broken glass in the bedroom and wait for the inevitable phone call.

Then, still wearing my navy blue suit because at any moment the police might arrive, I stretch out on our bed and listen to the rattle of the fan that sits on top of our bureau, groaning as it swivels left and right. My scarf flickers like a flame beside my face. A fly buzzes in through the broken window. I pull the sheet up over my head and let myself drift to sleep in the warm, blurry light.

By the time I wake, the room is dim and thick with the smell of yeast. I push my face into my pillow and think about Mrs. Knickerbocker. The odd woman meant well. Really, I should have invited her inside. Something soft and insistent nudges me. Half dreaming, I imagine sitting in an immaculate kitchen with Mrs. Knickerbocker, sipping coffee and swapping secrets—secrets that she would pat and knead until my heaviest worries turned buoyant as angel cake.

Something nudges me again, demanding more space on the bed. *Kevin?*

I kick aside the sheet. Not Kevin. The bread dough has swelled up out of the kitchen. It's made its way down the hall, and here it is in the bedroom, pushing against me like a drowsy lover. Moonlight shining through the broken window gives the steaming dough a luminescent glow. And the room—so silent. The dough has puffed up onto the bureau. It's wrapped itself around the fan and stopped the blades.

Finding my voice, I whisper, "Mrs. Knickerbocker, whatever did you put in that bread?"

Out in the living room, the phone lets out a smothered ring. *The hospital.* Or the police. When I leap from bed, the floor squishes beneath me. It's as soft as a pillow. I crawl on my knees and fumble over the dough. It oozes warmly between my fingers. The phone rings again. I try to stand. The floor moves like jelly. There's nothing I can do but crawl and then wriggle from the room, dizzy and nearly drunk from the smell of all that yeast.

Ringing, ringing, ringing—three more times. I shout, "Wait!" Before I can reach the phone, the answering machine clicks on and I hear the hollow recorded voice of my missing husband.

Hi! Kevin and Nadine aren't home, but we care about you. Please do leave us a message!

I wobble to my feet and tumble down the hall. The dough is everywhere. It sprawls across the coffee table. It drapes over Kevin's wing-backed chair. It squats like a plump white ottoman on top of the answering machine, which now echoes with Mrs. Knickerbocker's muffled voice: "Yoo—hooo—Nadine? Are you there?"

As I stumble across the cushion of her bread, I cry, "Here! I'm here!" and then, inches from the phone, I fall again. Face down, I mumble, "Don't hang up."

I think for sure she will until, swaying from side to side, I feel the fermenting dough beneath me rise, lifting me to the comfort of her words.

Hank

I was stretched out on the ceiling, sipping my morning coffee, when Sarah barged in, waving her arms and shrieking, "My Gawd! What happened?"

Leave it to Sarah to get hysterical. I told her to calm down. A bit of trouble with my gravity was all. Nothing to get exercised about.

But you know Sarah. She kept shoving food up to me, ordering me to eat. That woman was bound and determined to get me on the ground.

Sarah is my oldest girl, bossy as she can be. Not being able to fix my gravity made her near crazy. Of course, the heavy foods she gave me did no good. When a man's gravity is broke, it's broke, and nothing will weigh him down.

To tell the truth, losing your gravity isn't such a terrible thing. At first I was a bit dizzy. I clung tight to the ceiling fan (it don't work) and blinked down at the breakfast table. The sight of my buttered toast made my stomach flip over. Then I smelled the coffee. I reached to grab hold of my mug and began to sip.

The coffee helped settle me. I began to see that the ceiling was every bit as nice as the floor. Maybe the ceiling was even nicer, 'cause now I didn't have to work so hard at keeping my feet glued down. When my girl Sarah barged in, I knew that the ceiling was a damned good place to be.

There Sarah was, waving her arms and wagging her tongue. From where I was, Sarah looked upside down, like a bat hanging from a rafter. Later, after she tied me to the chair, and the chair drifted out the window, I couldn't help noticing that everything looked upside down. Cars, trucks, houses, and trees were all up-ended. Why, the whole damned world was upside down and—for the first time in my life—I felt right side up.

Gravity, shmavity!

Clara

Gifford seemed pale behind his high, dark desk. The cherry-framed mirror—*my mirror*—reflected the bald spot at the back of his head. The mirror also reflected his computer keyboard, a bowl of dusty lifesavers, and a coffee mug with a grinning monkey face. The mirror did *not* reflect me, which proves you can't trust a salesman.

I sipped coffee and eyed the carved cupid over the mirror. "Okay, say it."

Gifford leaned forward, a pasty hand on his pasty cheek.

"I know what you think about me, so there's no need to hold back."

Gifford rocked in his chair. Minutes—yes, they must have been full minutes—passed before he answered with the deliberate gentleness that might be used with a hysterical child. "What is it you think I think?"

Another trick. I lifted my chin. "If I say what I think you think, you'll think it's what I think."

Gifford waited, blinking his pallid eyes.

"I think you think I have a problem with mirrors."

"Well, I—" Reaching across the desk, he touched the back of my hand. "I can see you're upset."

So I blurted everything. I told about the lunch hours in the changing room at Porgett's, about the wall of empty mirrors there, about the salesman at Lord & Taylor, about the failed efforts to recover my reflection. "Everyone thinks it's so easy, but it's not. Not for me."

The room became unbearably hot. Why didn't he say something? Men are so condescending. I met his gaze with a glare. Finally, his lips moved. He wanted to know whether I'd been getting enough sleep, whether I'd been working too hard. Had he listened to me at all?

"You think you're so smart." I wobbled to my feet. "But this could happen to you."

Gifford extended his fleshy hands, palms up. The tips of his fingers seemed impossibly white—almost translucent.

"You could wake up and find it gone. Anyone could. Just like that."

"Clara—" He stood slowly. "I think you should know—"

"It's okay, Giff." I snatched up my coffee mug. "You can have my resignation." I was almost out the door when I threw one last glance at the carved cupid above the mirror (*my mirror!*) and in the dark corner of my peripheral vision, I caught a glimpse of red hair, an eyelash, a bright pink ear. "Who—?" When I approached, she rushed toward me, arm outstretched, and with a shock of recognition, I dropped my coffee mug. Well, not dropped exactly. The monkey face flew from my hands and somersaulted over Gifford's bald head. China crunched against glass.

"Oh!" One gasp and the mirror dissolved into shards. I dropped to my knees to collect them.

"Stop—" Gifford pulled at my elbow. "You'll cut yourself."

An eyebrow skidded under his desk. "Just let me get this—"

"Clara, stop. I want to tell you—"

Have you ever seen hair glisten like a glowworm? Have you ever tried to hold onto pure light? Have you ever cupped a piece of yourself in the palm of your hand? Then you'll understand why I wriggled from Gifford's hands and held onto the shard.

"Please. Clara—You're bleeding." Standing over me, his polished shoes sparkled with shattered glass and so did his legs, his sleeves, his navy blue tie.

I sat on the floor. The broken piece nestled between my fingers like a fuzzy caterpillar. "This is me," I told Gifford. "It's all that's left." I searched his eyes and they turned as translucent as his fingernails. I wasn't imagining this. He was fading.

By the time the ambulance arrived, Gifford was nothing more than ripple in the atmosphere, the breath of something he meant to say.

Elizabeth

We could barely see ourselves in the dim light of the changing room. Women leaned close to the mirrored wall. One poor soul tapped on the glass as though trying to adjust her image. In this murky light, my dress didn't look at all tacky. The sequins set off the highlights in my hair and the beading at the neckline glowed with a light that seemed impossible in this cramped and shadowed place. Blinking at my reflection, I decided that the silver dress would light a spark in anyone. Even Gifford.

Gifford had grown hazy and remote over the past few years. He drifted through the house like an old memory, his footsteps soft on the stairs. "Are you worried about the ad campaign?" I asked. He always used to say that a good ad is like poetry and that a single comma, properly placed, will make or break a sale.

He shrugged. "Such a lot of nonsense."

I had to face the truth: My husband, a big teddy bear of a man, beloved in business circles for his firm handshake and Santa Claus laugh, was fading.

Not all at once, of course. It started with his fingernails, which turned pale and then transparent, revealing pink skin and tiny veins at the tips of his fingers. I scarcely noticed the change until one evening at the circus benefit performance, I reached to clasp his hand and felt only the smooth gold wedding band. Then, as I pressed it, this also dissolved. Groping in the dark, I found—*nothing!*

"*Gifford!*" I called to him over the toots of a calliope. "What in the name of heaven—?"

"*Shhh—!*" He refused to materialize until the aerialist finished her high-wire performance and somersaulted into a pretzel-shaped bow. The amphitheater exploded with applause.

"That's more like it," I said. During the encore—a clumsy juggling act—I squeezed his warm hand to keep him from wafting away.

After that night, the lapses came more often. He melted into the steam of his coffee mug. He flickered in front of the TV. Sometimes I'd walk into a room and catch him reading the newspaper without his nose, which tended to recede into his mustache when he felt fatigued.

"Whatever are you thinking of when you go off like that?" I asked.

I wondered if he blamed me for pushing him all these years, for pressuring him to finish his MBA when he wanted to study literature. I suspected that he resented me for organizing charity events when our daughter Julie had troubles of her own. And then there were those noisy dinner parties where I served, God help me, sushi.

Trembling back into focus, he said, "I don't believe I'm thinking of anything."

Mind you, he enjoyed stretches of clarity. For weeks on end, Gifford seemed as sharply tuned as you and me—a hefty man, possessing all his parts except for the hair that used to curl over his high, shiny brow. But even on his best days his voice blurred, sentences ending in ellipses or question marks, and I sensed that he'd vanish completely unless I reached him soon.

And so on the evening of our twenty-fifth wedding anniversary—our *silver* anniversary—I slithered into the sequin dress and hurried out onto our bedroom balcony. Gifford had just returned from his office. He stood in the gardens below. Darkness seeped between the branches of the hydrangea bushes and what must have been a thousand fireflies made silent explosions in the shadows. Stepping much too gently for a man his size, he walked soundlessly to the edge of the swimming pool and, standing at the deep end, set his briefcase on the diving board. Then he stood oddly still, gazing at the dark water that glistened in the light of a pale and lopsided moon.

Even from the height of the balcony, I could smell the chlorine of the pool mingle with the heavy scent of his cologne. Nearly sick with longing, I waited for Gifford to turn and smile up at me, to say something—anything. But as I watched him, willing him to turn around, he fogged over.

Could he tell that he was fading? Did he feel a flutter in his stomach, a weakness in his knees, a whistle of wind beneath his skin? When he looked at his hands, could he see that his flesh had turned translucent? Was he frightened by the sight of his own blue veins?

Twenty-five years of marriage and I couldn't answer these questions. Shimmering on the balcony, I wondered if he even remembered our special day.

"*Giff—*"

His hand pressed against his lapel, he turned and gazed up and—for the first time—I saw what appeared to be a rose, which, although only half open, blazed with magnificent intensity.

He did remember! Like a teenage girl, I rattled down the narrow wrought iron stairway. Astonished fireflies swooped from the bushes and hovered overhead, twinkling. Startled by this sudden gust of brilliance, I caught a heel in the grate of the bottom step. With a swish of sequins, I fell into—and through—Gifford's waiting arms.

I stumbled to my feet and fumbled for him, but the Gifford who stood before me, palms outstretched, was no more than a ripple in the atmosphere, a mirage in a gray suit and striped silk tie, and when I reached again, the suit evaporated, leaving only the purple sheen of his lungs and the pink, pulsing thing I'd mistaken for a rose. It was, of course, only his heart.

Mrs. Knickerbocker

A lot of you've been asking my recipe so here it is. Mind you, this bread isn't exact. It starts with basics like flour, milk, and freckles and takes off from there. All's you do is mix your ingredients and let them sit. By and by the batter will puff up and start a life its own. Pat it like a baby's bottom. Stir in some extra bits, if you want—a finger, an eyebrow, a tooth. Pinch off a belly button (no more) and give it room. Take another pinch and do the same. Then take a pinch from that pinch. Don't knead. No matter how much your fingers itch, you've got to give each piece time to bubble and swell.

Waiting is the hard part. Some people get nervous and fiddle. Or they worry about flies and they cover the bowl too tight. Or they fret about the toenails going bad and they stick the batter in the fridge.

If you're one of those particular ones, you best stay out of the kitchen for a spell. With this bread you don't want to fuss. It's like this. For the batter to rise, everything's got to go sour.

Jackie Craven has work published in *Berkeley Fiction Review, Limestone, Mid-American Review, New Ohio Review, Nimrod International Journal, Water-Stone Review,* and many other journals. She also writes about architecture and is the author of two books on interior design. She completed her Doctor of Arts in Writing from the University at Albany, New York. Visit her at www.JackieCraven.com.